A NOTE TO PARENTS

Disney's First Readers Level 3 books were developed for children who have mastered many basic reading skills and are on the road to becoming competent and confident readers.

Disney's First Readers Level 3 books have more fully developed plots, introduce harder words, and use more complex sentence and paragraph structures than Level 2 books.

Reading is the single most important way a young person learns to enjoy reading. Give your child opportunities to read many different types of literature. Make books, magazines, and writing materials available to your child. Books that are of special interest to your child will motivate more reading and provide more enjoyment. Here are some additional tips to help you spend quality reading time with your child:

★ Promote thinking skills. Ask if your child liked the story or not and why. This is one of the best ways to learn if your child understood what he or she has read.

★ Continue to read aloud. No matter how old the child may be, or how proficient a reader, hearing a delightful story read aloud is still exciting and a very important part of becoming a more fluent reader.

★ Read together on a regular basis, and encourage your child to read to you often. Be a good teacher by being a good listener and audience!

★ Praise all reading efforts, no matter how small.

★ Try out the After-Reading Fun activities at the end of each book to enhance the skills your child has already learned.

Remember that early-reading experiences that you share with your child can help him or her to become a confident and successful reader later on!

— Patricia Koppman
Past President
International Reading Association

For my father
—J. K.

Paints and pencils by Sol Studios

First published by Disney Press, New York, New York.
This edition published by Scholastic Inc.,
90 Old Sherman Turnpike, Danbury, Connecticut 06816
by arrangement with Disney Licensed Publishing.

SCHOLASTIC and associated logos are trademarks of Scholastic Inc.

ISBN 0-7172-6466-1

Printed in the U.S.A.

BUZZ AND THE BUBBLE PLANET

by Judy Katschke
Illustrated by Sol Studios

Disney's First Readers — Level 3
A Story from Disney's *Toy Story*

SCHOLASTIC INC.

New York   Toronto   London   Auckland   Sydney
Mexico City   New Delhi   Hong Kong   Buenos Aires

A new toy in Andy's room could mean fun—or it could mean trouble!
"It looks like a spaceship!" Woody said.

Buzz Lightyear hopped off Andy's bed. "Did someone say 'spaceship'?" he asked.

Buzz climbed into the cockpit. "I'm taking this baby for a test run!" he cried.

"Be careful, Buzz," Woody warned. "You're not real. You're a toy!"

"So is this spaceship," Buzz said.
"It's a match made in heaven!"

"I want to help," Hamm said. He took
a piece of paper from the box. It was
the instructions.

"I don't need instructions!" Buzz cried.

Woody knocked on the spaceship.
"Buzz, this is a bad idea!" he cried.

But Woody goofed. He hit the ON
switch by mistake!

The spaceship began to shake.

"Ready for liftoff!" Buzz shouted.

Whoosh! The ship blasted out the door . . . and began to fall!

"Oh no!" cried Buzz. "I'm going to crash!"

The ship fell down and Buzz went flying out . . .

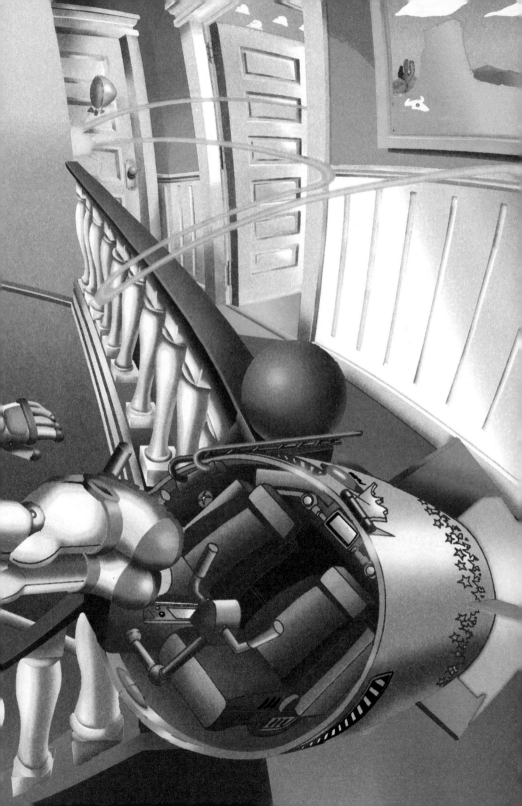

. . . and splash-landed inside a deep crater full of water.

Buzz was not hurt. He slowly peeked out and looked around.

"I seem to have crash-landed on a strange planet!" Buzz said.

He jumped out of the crater. Suddenly, the water was sucked into a hole.

"Now that's what I call infinity and beyond!" Buzz said.

Buzz felt like he was light-years away from Andy's room.

"How will I get back home without my spaceship?" he wondered.

Buzz decided to make the best of it. He would explore this strange planet. "I may be a toy," Buzz said, "but I'm still Buzz Lightyear, space ranger!"

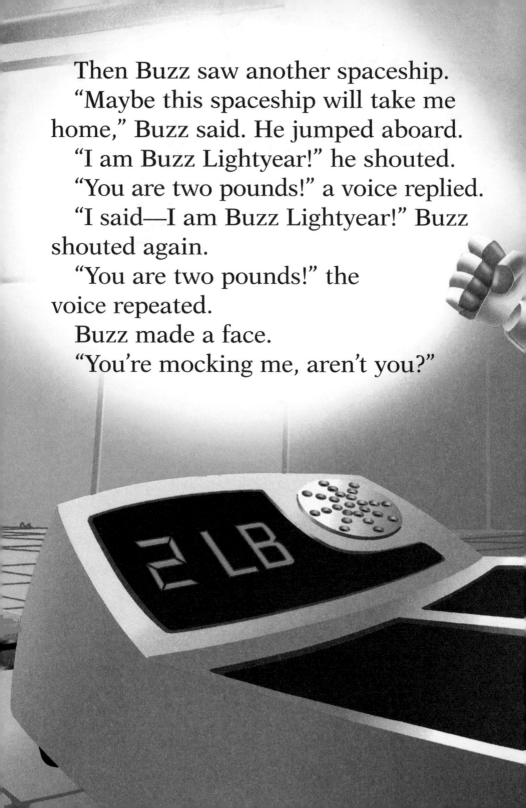

Then Buzz saw another spaceship.
"Maybe this spaceship will take me home," Buzz said. He jumped aboard.
"I am Buzz Lightyear!" he shouted.
"You are two pounds!" a voice replied.
"I said—I am Buzz Lightyear!" Buzz shouted again.
"You are two pounds!" the voice repeated.
Buzz made a face.
"You're mocking me, aren't you?"

Back in Andy's room, Woody
held a meeting.

"How will we find Buzz?" he asked.

"I'll send out the troops!" Sarge said.
"Fall in, soldiers!" he shouted.

"I wish I could roar like that,"
Rex sighed.

Meanwhile, Buzz was wrestling a strange robot. The robot shook and whirred. It tickled Buzz all over!

Buzz pressed a yellow dot on the robot's neck. The robot stopped moving.

"Whew!" Buzz said. "That was a close brush with danger!"

Buzz's brush with the robot had him all shook-up. But he didn't give up. He kept on exploring the planet.

Strange things kept happening.
Buzz fought strong winds!
He skidded on slippery meteorites!
He was attacked by strange globs
of blue slime!

Then Buzz found Andy's cat on a heap of cosmic clouds!

"The aliens here have captured Whiskers!" Buzz gasped. "Don't worry, Whiskers! Buzz Lightyear to the rescue!"

"PHHHHFFFFFT!" Whiskers hissed. She flicked her tail at Buzz.

Buzz flew through space once again.
Thump! Buzz landed inside a bright
red boat.

"This planet's surface is wobbly,"
Buzz said. "And so is my tummy!"

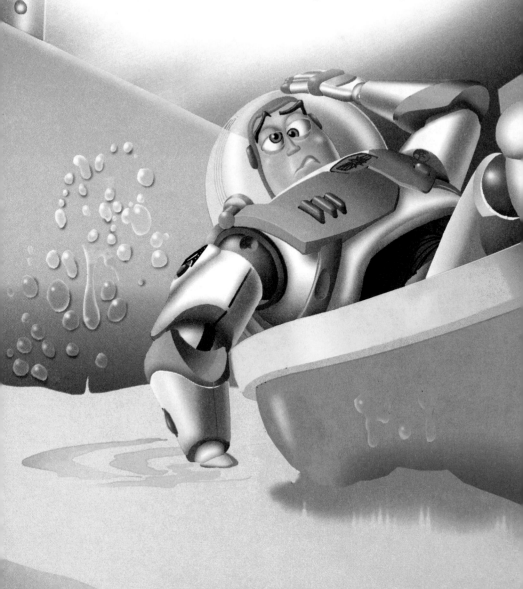

Buzz saw a gang of yellow creatures.
"Alien life-forms!" Buzz cried. "Who is your leader?"
"Squeak!" they replied.
"What a strange name," Buzz said.

Buzz drifted away. Soon he saw a
happy face and the words:
        Squeakyclean Bubbles
"You must be Squeak!" Buzz shouted.
"I am Buzz Lightyear. I come in peace."

Boing! Buzz's wings opened.
They hit Squeak. The aliens' leader
began to fall!

Buzz watched as thick pink goo
poured from Squeak's head. The goo
turned into hundreds and hundreds
of bubbles around Buzz.

"I am under attack!" Buzz cried.

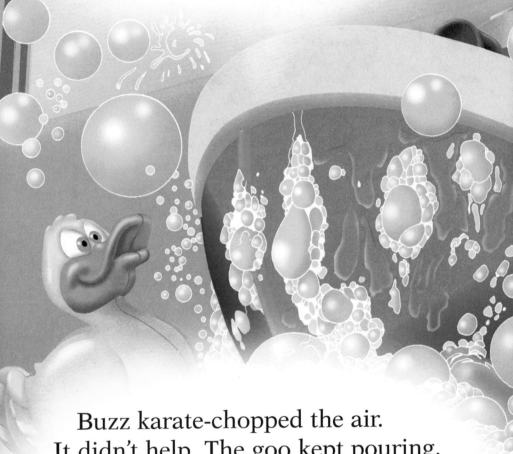

Buzz karate-chopped the air.
It didn't help. The goo kept pouring.
The bubbles kept coming and coming!

"Hai-yaaa!" Buzz shouted. "Back,
you beastly blobs!"

Sarge and his troops were nearby.
"We have located the spaceship!"
Sarge whispered into his walkie-talkie.

"Where's Buzz?" Woody asked.

"In the bathroom!" Sarge answered.
"Should we save him?"

Rex looked out the window.

"Here comes Andy," Rex called.
"And he looks really dirty."

Woody smiled. "Help is on the
way, Sarge!"

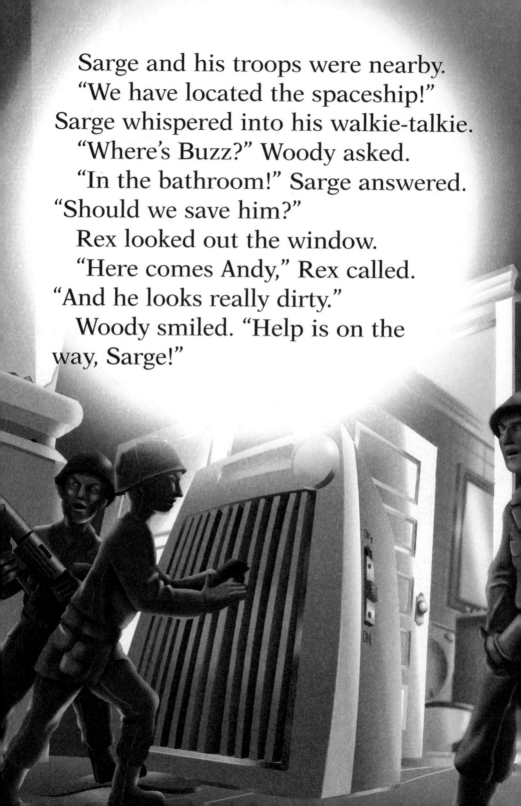

Back on the Bubble Planet, Buzz
was in real trouble. Bubble goo was
everywhere. Aliens were all around
him. Buzz was losing his hold. Soon he
would fall into Squeak's bubbly trap.

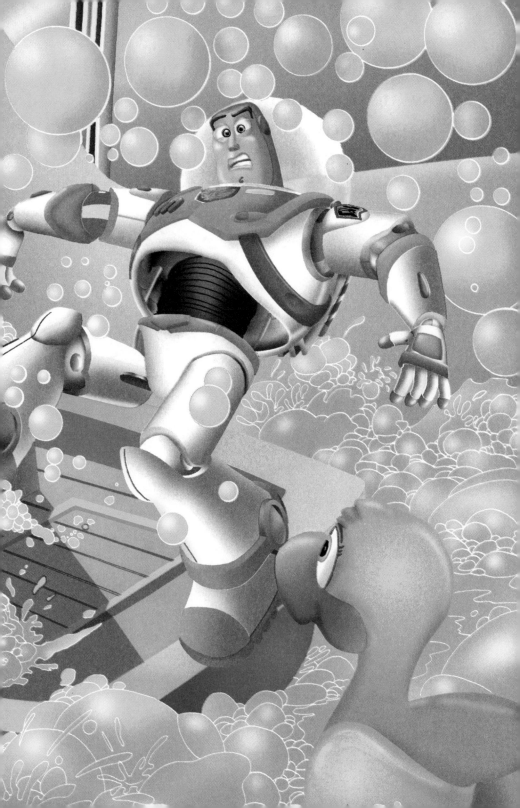

Suddenly, Buzz heard a voice: "Hey! How did you get in here?"

It was Andy! He lifted Buzz into the air. "This tub ain't big enough for the two of us," Andy said in his best cowboy voice.

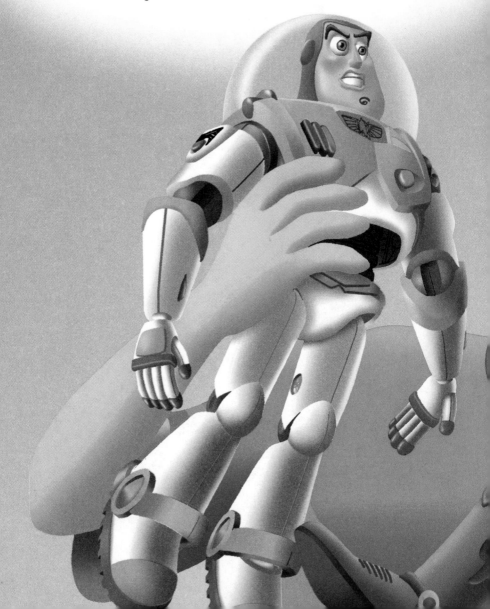

"But it IS big enough for the THREE of us!"

Buzz looked at his friends and smiled. He was a lot closer to home than he had thought.

. . . And a lot cleaner, too!

AFTER-READING FUN

Enhance the reading experience with follow-up questions to help your child develop reading comprehension and increase his/her awareness of words.

Approach this with a sense of play. Make a game of having your child answer the questions. You do not need to ask all the questions at one time. Let these questions be fun discussions rather than a test. If your child doesn't have instant recall, encourage him/her to look back into the book to "research" the answers. You'll be modeling what good readers do and, at the same time, forging a sharing bond with your child.

BUZZ AND THE BUBBLE PLANET

1. What was the new toy in Andy's room?

2. In what room of the house did Buzz land?

3. What is the strange robot that Buzz encounters?

4. Why did Buzz's tummy feel "wobbly"?

5. How many different kinds of transportation can you name?

6. How many three-syllable words can you find in the story?

Answers: 1. a spaceship. **2.** the bathroom. **3.** an electric toothbrush. **4.** he felt seasick. **5.** *possible answers:* bicycle, motorcycle, train, plane, car, truck, sailboat, submarine. **6.** *possible answers:* instructions, slippery, aliens, located, suddenly, and another.